D1589270

C334479466

ORCHARD BOOKS

First published in the USA by Scholastic Inc in 2020
First published in the UK in 2020 by The Watts Publishing Group

1 3 5 7 9 8 6 4 2

A CIP catalogue record for this book is available from the British
Library.

ISBN 978 1 40836 286 0

Printed and bound in Great Britain by Clays Ltd, Elcograf S.p.A

MIX
Paper from
responsible sources
FSC® C104740

The paper and board used in this book are
made from wood from responsible sources.

Orchard Books
An imprint of Hachette Children's Group
Part of The Watts Publishing Group Limited
Carmelite House, 50 Victoria Embankment, London EC4Y 0DZ

An Hachette UK Company

www.hachette.co.uk
www.hachettechildrens.co.uk

POKÉMON UNKNOWN

Adapted by Jeanette Lane

ORCHARD

CHAPTER 1
ASH'S DREAM

"Come on, Ash, get up!" Rotom Dex cried, jetting around the bungalow in alarm. "You have to get out of bed, eat breakfast and head off to school!" Rotom Dex pleaded, but Ash only snorted and snored. Rotom Dex liked for everyone to stick to the morning routine. But that morning, Ash had slept late.

Ash had been staying with Professor Kukui for a while. The professor's cosy bungalow on the island of Melemele had become his home away from home. Melemele was a tropical island in the Alola region with all kinds of new Pokémon to discover, so Ash couldn't be happier. Plus, Professor Kukui was an amazing host. Not only was the professor a top Pokémon researcher and a great teacher, he was also a good cook!

But Ash wasn't going to have time to eat breakfast if he didn't hurry …

"You need to wake up, too, Pikachu!" Rotom Dex poked at the sleepy Electric-type Pokémon. Lycanroc nudged Ash with its cold nose. Ash and Pikachu didn't show any signs of waking up soon.

Ash had a very good reason for not waking up. He was in the middle of a bizarre and spooky dream. In the dream, Ash was exploring an ancient altar. Two very rare Pokémon appeared, and they were trying to tell Ash something. It was so dark and misty, Ash couldn't see well, but it

all seemed very real.

"Wake up, Rowlet!" Rotom Dex howled at the feathered Pokémon that cooed in its sleep. What was wrong with everyone?

"I understand, Solgaleo," Ash mumbled under his breath, his eyes still closed. "I promise, Lunala."

"He's still talking in his sleep," Rotom Dex said, disgusted. "Litten, you're up next." Rotom Dex hoped the Fire-type Pokémon would have more luck waking Ash.

Litten jumped at the chance. "*Mrrrrrow!*" With its claws out, Litten pounced on Ash's belly and then flicked its furry tail in Ash's face, again and again. "*Mrrrowrowrow!*"

Ash sat up, gasping. His eyes were red and his face puffy, but he was awake!

"I keep thinking about the most incredible dream I had," he said as he pulled on his clothes. "At least I think I did." Ash tried to tug the details of the dream from the back of his mind. "I promise," he said to himself. "What did I promise?"

As he and the Pokémon – Pikachu, Rowlet, Litten and Lycanroc – ate breakfast, Ash mulled over the foggy flashes of his dream. He couldn't recall many details, but he felt like it was important. It felt like something amazing had happened at that altar. If only he could remember!

Even though Ash and Pikachu rushed through breakfast, they still needed to hurry to get to school on time. They were running up a hill when Pikachu suddenly stopped.

"*Pika, pika?*" Pikachu glanced into the forest next to the path.

"What's up, Pikachu?" Ash wondered out loud, but his companion just darted into the dark forest.

"*Pika, pi pi pi.*" Pikachu sprinted down the path. Ash took off, too, his backpack banging against his back.

"Where are you going?" Rotem Dex cried, still on the road.

"Hey, Pikachu!" Ash called out, trying to track down his friend. "Wait up!"

"Ash, stop!" Rotom Dex shouted, zooming close behind. "Where are you going?"

When Ash saw Pikachu in a small clearing, he skidded to a stop. Suddenly, he understood why Pikachu ran off.

"Tapu Koko!" Ash blurted. With its brilliant orange feathers and bold black-and-white markings, Tapu Koko was easy to see, even in the dark shadows of the leafy trees. Tapu Koko hovered in the thick air. It seemed to stare down at Ash, Pikachu and Rotom Dex. Ash could hardly believe that he was seeing the secretive Guardian of Melemele Island again.

Suddenly, Tapu Koko zoomed straight up in the air, through the branches and out of sight. Tapu Koko was always mysterious, but Ash was still stunned. "*Now what?*" he wondered.

The forest was silent, but then there was a tiny sound in the grass.

Ash, Pikachu and Rotom Dex crept toward it, and nestled in the grass they found a small, glowing Pokémon. It cooed in its sleep. It wasn't a Pokémon that Ash had ever seen before. Its body was shaped like an indigo-and-lilac-coloured cloud, with two bright blue circles for cheeks. Its two stubby arms had blue clouds for fists, with a white starlike pattern. The little Pokémon looked so peaceful, breathing deeply.

"A Pokémon?" Ash said under his breath.

Pikachu nuzzled the little Pokémon with its yellow nose. The snoozing Pokémon giggled.

"*Pika.*" Pikachu seemed to like it!

"It's still asleep," Ash observed, leaning down. He reached out and picked it up. "It's so light," Ash said. Then, without thinking, he mumbled, "I promised." A chill ran down Ash's spine, and a wave of emotions

overcame him.

"I promised!" he shouted out loud. "I'm starting to remember now. I promised that I'd find you!" He was talking to the strange, new Pokémon.

Rotom Dex was shocked. "You made a promise? When? Where? Whom did you make it with?" it asked.

"It was last night, when I had a dream,"

Ash started to explain. He struggled to remember more. "With somebody."

"Illogical! Illogical! Illogical!" Rotom Dex insisted.

The new Pokémon stirred in Ash's arms. Its black face and thin pink mouth twitched.

"*It* must be having a dream. I wonder what kind of Pokémon it is," Ash said.

From over Ash's shoulder, Rotom Dex answered with certainty. "You just leave the data research to me." But, instead of its screen lighting up with a picture of the cute little Pokémon, Rotom Dex's screen showed three question marks. "Now, that's unusual! My research doesn't contain any Pokémon data for it at all!"

CHAPTER 2
MEET NEBBY

Meanwhile, at the Pokémon School, everyone noticed that Ash was late.

"Isn't that odd?" Professor Kukui commented from the front of the classroom. "He left the house a while before I did."

"Sidetracked, maybe?" Kiawe suggested, staring at Ash's empty seat. The expert Fire-type Pokémon Trainer knew Ash well.

"When it comes to Ash, anything is possible," Lillie pointed out.

"I'll guess he's trying to catch a Pokémon somewhere," Sophocles added. Ash's classmates all knew how much Ash loved a Pokémon adventure!

Just then, they heard footsteps pounding down the hall. In no time, Ash appeared in the doorway. Pikachu and Rotom Dex were hot on his tail. Ash ran right up to his teacher, panting. "Professor Kukui!"

"We've discovered a Pokémon not in my database!" Rotom Dex announced.

"It was the one I saw in a dream last night!" Ash exclaimed. "I dreamt I made a promise to somebody that I'd find it and take care of it, and then … and then … and then …" He paused, gasping for breath. Ash then pounded his head in frustration. "Why do people forget their dreams?" he asked, annoyed.

Professor Kukui put his hand on Ash's shoulder. "All right," he reassured him. "Calm down a bit and tell me more about this Pokémon. Where is it now?"

"It's here in my bag," Ash said, shifting the backpack off his shoulder. Everyone rushed over and crowded around. They all leaned forwards to peek into Ash's bag.

At once, the new Pokémon rose up in the air, just over the kids' heads.

"It floats," Ash pointed out.

"But it's asleep," Rotom Dex added, amazed.

Pikachu, Popplio, Togedemaru, Snowy, Steenee and Marowak all mumbled in excitement. It wasn't every day they met an unknown Pokémon!

"What a cutie!" Mallow said.

"It doesn't appear at all in this book," Lillie said with a slight frown. She was holding the fully updated guide to all Pokémon. "What a mystery."

Professor Oak, the principal, had walked into the room and was observing the scene.

"Do you have any clues, Professor Oak?" Professor Kukui asked.

"Well, it's one I've never come across before," he admitted. "But it gives me such a … *Sigil-lift!*" No one paid much attention to Principal Oak's joke. They were all too interested in the unknown Pokémon.

"We could be looking at a brand-new kind of Pokémon," Sophocles said hopefully.

"And if that's true, Ash is the one who made the discovery," Kiawe pointed out.

"Really, I did?!" said Ash. He liked that idea!

"I say we do everything we can to investigate this new Pokémon!" Professor Kukui was almost as excited as his students!

Meanwhile, the Pokémon was still floating in the air, snoozing away.

"Man, you can sleep through just about anything!" Ash remarked. As if in response, the Pokémon laughed while its eyes were still closed.

"It's giggling," said Lana. "How cute is that?"

"Just like a baby," Mallow agreed.

Ash overheard Lillie. She was mumbling
to herself. "Nebula, Nebby …"

"Why Nebby?" Ash asked.

Lillie regarded the levitating Pokémon
again. "It seems to have stars glittering
inside it. And see how it floats like a

cloud?" she said. "Well, since a *nebula* is the word for a cloud of gas with stars inside, I was thinking, why don't we name it Nebby?"

Ash smiled. "It's like a miniature nebula. Great name! Yeah, let's call it Nebby."

Lillie seemed happy and surprised that he agreed.

"That name's not bad!" Kiawe added.

"Well, I like the name Purple Sweet Cotton Candy better," Sophocles admitted, "but Nebby will do!"

"Nebby is a fantastic name," Mallow said with gusto. The others nodded in agreement.

"Then it's decided," Professor Kukui announced.

Lillie let out a happy giggle and said, "Little Nebby." Her voice was almost a whisper, but Nebby immediately woke up … and started crying! Nebby's wails grew louder and louder.

Not only was it screeching, but tears were gushing out of its eyes in steady streams.

Ash tried to take the little Pokémon in his arms, but Nebby kept crying. Ash rocked it, patted it, swung it from side to side. Nothing worked.

"It's like a thousand painful Supersonics!" Rotom Dex whined, covering his ears.

"Don't cry, Nebby," Ash tried to reassure it. "You're such a big Pokémon! Don't cry, don't cry!" When nothing soothed the little Pokémon, Ash gave up. "You deal with this," he demanded,

shoving Nebby into Kiawe's arms. "Thanks! Bye!"

Kiawe froze. Nebby was still crying – loudly! Kiawe didn't know how to stop it! "I DON'T KNOW WHAT TO DO!" he shouted.

Then Kiawe took a deep breath. He looked down at the purple Pokémon with the cloud-shaped arms. "When I sang this to Mimo, she stopped crying every time," he said. He began to sing a lullaby, but Nebby still wailed. "I can't take it any more," he declared. "Mallow, please help me out. TAKE IT!" Kiawe thrust Nebby into Mallow's arms.

"Let's see," Mallow said, feeling nervous. Her eyes grew wide. "There, Nebby, Nebby,

Nebby … no need to cry!" she said. She gave the Pokémon a hug. "We're all friends!"

Almost immediately, Nebby calmed down. All the other Pokémon peeked out, hoping that Nebby had stopped. When the little Pokémon saw the others, it giggled. Its mood was now all happy and bright.

"Look at it laughing right after it was crying. Just like a baby!" Ash said, relieved.

"Now that we've gotten Nebby in a good mood, how about we find out what it likes to eat," Professor Kukui suggested. "We can't expect to take care of Nebby if we don't know that!"

"Yeah!" the Pokémon School students all said. Then they put together a table full of lots of different food options.

"Nebby? Do any of these look yummy to you?" Ash asked. All the students and Pokémon were gathered around.

Nebby floated over the table, looking at the bowls. Each was full of something that looked a lot like dog food – brown and mushy.

"How about this? It's soft and has a mild flavour and nutritionally speaking, it should perfectly suit a little Pokémon's growing needs." Lillie pointed to a light-brown option.

"Sounds good," Ash said. "How's this?" He held it up to Nebby, but the Pokémon refused to eat it – and refused to eat any of the other brown stuff in the bowls. Next, the students all started to offer food out of their own lunches. Sandwiches, salads, cake, milk, anything! But Nebby refused it all.

"Hey, maybe you might like this," Sophocles said, holding up a bright blue nugget. "Star candy!" Ash held a piece of the candy up to Nebby, and the Pokémon gobbled it up.

"It likes them!" Rotom Dex announced.

"Since star candy is shaped like stars, it suits Nebby to a T!" Lillie pointed out. "What a big relief."

"I'm so glad we finally found something it likes to eat," Principal Oak said.

"We're going to need to stock up on it back at our place," Professor Kukui said.

Sophocles handed over his bag of candy, and he also promised to take Ash to a market that had lots of star candy. They agreed to go after school. Lillie had a driver who picked her up from school, so she offered to give them a lift.

That afternoon, after Ash had bought a supply of star candy, the three friends headed home. The driver dropped off Sophocles first.

"See ya!" Ash called out.

"Bye-bye, guys," Sophocles said as he opened the car door.

"Until later!" Lillie said with a wave. The driver headed to Professor Kukui's house next.

It had been a long day. "What's that?" Ash murmured when he saw a helicopter in the distance. He didn't think much about it then, but he'd soon learn that that helicopter was headed for Professor Kukui's place. Ash was in for a surprise

when he arrived home; the news of his
Nebby discovery had already travelled
beyond Melemele Island.

CHAPTER 3

SPECIAL GUESTS

"Welcome home," Professor Kukui greeted Ash as he got out of the car.

"Hey, Professor," Ash replied.

Professor Kukui took a breath and looked at his young student. "So, Ash ... we have some guests who say they want to see you," he said.

Ash paused. Who would want to see him?

"That's you *and* Nebby," the professor clarified. "And you, too, Lillie."

Lillie was still seated in the car. Snowy was sitting on her lap, all nice and cosy. "Why would they want to see me?" Lillie wondered out loud, opening the car door. But the answer was obvious as soon as she and Ash stepped into Professor Kukui's house. There was a group of people there, and sitting closest to the door was a tall woman with blonde hair that fell to her knees like a shimmering waterfall.

"Mother!" Lillie exclaimed.

"Lillie!" The woman stood up at once and turned to Lillie, her arms wide open.

"*Mother?*" Ash asked, shocked. "You mean," he stammered, "y-you're Lillie's mum?"

"*Pika?*"

"Yes! Lillie is my daughter!" she exclaimed.

Well, that explained why the guests wanted to see Lillie. But Ash was curious why they had asked to see him – and Nebby.

"How's my baby?" Lillie's mum said. She seemed delighted to see her daughter. She swooped in and tried to give Lillie a hug.

Lillie did not seem delighted. "I'm not a baby," Lillie insisted, dodging out of the way. "I wish you'd stop embarrassing me."

"See, now that's my cute little girl. Don't forget, you'll always be my sweet little baby!" This time, Lillie's mum captured her daughter with her long, thin arms and gave her a great big bear hug.

"I wasn't born yesterday!" Lillie tried to pull away.

"Lillie! Is that a ..." her mum began,

but then paused. "You're able to touch Pokémon now, aren't you?! Good baby! Good baby!" She ruffled Lillie's hair.

Lillie rolled her green eyes. "What part of 'stop embarrassing me' don't you get?"

"Lillie raised Snowy from an Egg," Rotom Dex pointed out. "Very impressive."

"From an Egg? My baby raised a hatchling?" Her mum *was* impressed.

Lillie took a deep breath, then it all came out in a giant huff. "I keep telling you I am not a baby! Honestly!" She pushed her mum away. "You are always putting your own feelings first, never once thinking about how I might feel!"

Lillie's mum gasped. "That was never my intention," she replied.

But Lillie wasn't finished. She held Snowy

tight in one arm and pointed at her mum with the other. "It's just like with Clefairy!"

"Clefairy?" her mum asked.

"Remember when you made Clefairy evolve into Clefable when I wasn't even there?" Lillie said. "Using a Moon Stone?!"

"Uh, maybe ..." Lillie's mum's long hair draped over her face, hiding her expression.

"I wanted to keep Clefairy as a Clefairy, but you refused to listen to me!" Lillie complained.

"Still," Lillie's mum tried to explain, "I was the one training Clefairy! And the entire reason you wanted to keep it as Clefairy was because it was cute that way, and that didn't make any sense."

"It was cute that way," Lillie protested.

"That was the result of a decision based on a perfectly logical thought process."

Ash felt kind of embarrassed. He was overhearing what seemed like a private discussion between Lillie and her mum, but they were arguing in front of everyone! "Lillie's a lot more energetic when her mother's around, don't you think?" Ash whispered.

"Definitely," Professor Kukui agreed.

"And the similarities!" Rotom Dex pointed out. "Like their hair." They both had long, straight hair, in an unbelievably pale shade of blonde. But Lillie had a fringe, so her hair never shielded her face.

"They're both no-nonsense," said one of the women who had arrived with Lillie's mum.

"Professor Burnet?!" Rotom Dex blurted when it recognised the woman. She had a distinctive, sporty look, with curly white hair. She wore a grey sleeveless top and other on-the-go gear.

"You've changed form to a Pokédex!" the woman replied. "I'm honoured you know my name."

"I saw her on the morning news!" Rotom Dex explained to the others.

It was true! The woman was Professor Burnet, who had just won a Woman of the Year Award for the whole Alola region. The announcement had been on the news. Professor Burnet was a famous scientist who researched many things – including the existence of rare and ancient Pokémon. Professor Kukui had met her before, since they were both researchers.

"Let me introduce you all," Professor Kukui said. "This is Professor Burnet. She is an Aether Foundation researcher. And the President of Aether Foundation is Lusamine, Lillie's mother."

"It's nice to meet you," Lusamine said. She smiled at everyone. She spoke quickly, but her voice was warm. "Now please meet my team. Without them, the foundation couldn't do its work!" She motioned to the two people next to Professor Burnet. "Wicke and Faba."

"Alola, kids," said a young woman with purple hair and an eager grin. "My name's Wicke and I'm vice-chief for the Aether Foundation. It's a pleasure to meet you."

"And my name's Faba," said the man with

large lime-green-tinted glasses and a tiny, pointy beard. "I serve as the Aether Foundation's branch chief."

"This may be rushed," Lusamine said, leaning in close to Ash and Lillie, "but please introduce us to Nebby! Would you mind?" She clasped her hands together hopefully.

Ash stared at Lusamine. It did seem rushed, and it made Ash feel nervous. How did everyone at the Aether Foundation know about Nebby?

CHAPTER 4

ULTRA BEASTS

Even though Ash was shocked, he couldn't say no. Lillie's mum seemed nice, and, more importantly, she was Lillie's mum.

It was funny. Ash hadn't really ever thought about his classmates' parents. It was cool that Lillie's mum was the head of a gigantic foundation. Even better, the mission of the Aether Foundation was to help Pokémon. That made sense, because Lillie was always very helpful and she cared so much about all Pokémon. She was always reading about Pokémon and sharing the information in a helpful way. She could recite facts like an encyclopedia – or a Pokédex!

That's why it had been so weird that Lillie couldn't touch Pokémon. For a long time, she was not able to touch any Pokémon at all. Her special relationship with Snowy had changed that.

Lusamine liked Nebby at once, and it seemed like Nebby liked her back. She tickled it between the eyes and the young Pokémon giggled in its sleep.

"As I thought," Lusamine whispered. "It seems to be an Ultra Beast."

"An Ultra Beast?" Ash asked, feeling uncertain. He had never heard anyone use that term before.

"Please look at this," Professor Burnet said as she took a seat at one of Professor Kukui's computers. An image appeared on the large screen.

It was some kind of ancient mural that pictured some Pokémon Ash knew and many he did not. But one was very familiar. "It's Tapu Koko!" Ash called out.

"A long, long time ago," Professor Burnet explained, "some very odd creatures from another world appeared, and they challenged the Island Guardians to a terrible, wide-ranging battle. Have you ever heard that legend before?"

"I read everything about it in one of my books!" Lillie said. "And if I remember correctly, those odd creatures from another world are called Ultra Beasts."

"So my little baby is really studying!" Lusamine exclaimed. "I'm so happy that I enrolled you in Pokémon School!"

"You didn't enrol me," Lillie insisted, diving away from another of her mum's overwhelming hugs. "It was totally my idea to enrol there in the first place!"

Lusamine tapped her mouth with one finger. "I remember it differently," she said.

Ash wanted to get to the facts. "So you really think that Nebby is one of these Ultra Beasts?" he asked.

"It's statistically likely," Professor Burnet

replied.

"Any physical element with some sort of close relation to that other world, as well as the Ultra Beasts themselves, emits something that resembles a kind of aura," Faba said, pushing his giant glasses back into place. "And, our lab constantly measures it. Now, Wicke, please?"

"Right!" Wicke dived in and began to type on the keyboard. "Last night, we measured an enormous spike in the aura's power, in the vicinity of the Altar of the Sunne, located on Poni Island." As she typed, the image of a stone altar appeared on the screen.

"And just a little while ago—" Faba began, but Ash cut him off.

"That's the place!" Ash shouted, pointing

at the screen. It was all coming back to him!

Everyone looked at him. "What do you mean?" Professor Kukui asked.

"What place, Ash?" asked Rotom Dex.

"I remember," Ash stated. "That's where I was in my dream. Also, there were two really cool-looking Pokémon that appeared from out of the sky, Solgaleo and Lunala. And right after that, Nebby appeared from a blinding light …"

"Solgaleo?" Professor Kukui repeated.

"Lunala," repeated Professor Burnet. Both professors were clearly perplexed.

"Lusamine?!" Wicke said, looking to her boss for answers.

"Those are names that we know only by what we've learned through legends," Lusamine told them. "And now they've appeared to Ash!" Lusamine was clearly excited that Ash had encountered the Pokémon of lore in his dreams. She went on to tell them that she had been fascinated by Ultra Beasts since she was a child. Her father had told her stories about them.

Faba was not as easily convinced by Ash. He scowled. "It's a dream! A child's fancy!" he blurted.

But now, after hearing about Ash's dream, Lusamine seemed more interested in Nebby than ever. "Ash, of course, you'll allow the Aether Foundation to look after Nebby. Won't you?"

Ash was surprised by her question.

Wicke was quick to offer an explanation. "The Aether Foundation has an entire institution that houses Pokémon with the utmost respect, love and care," she assured Ash. "You can rest easy knowing it's in good hands!"

"Yeah, but ..."

"*Pika.*"

"But what?" Lusamine prompted him.

She was certain that the foundation was the best place for the newly discovered Pokémon.

"I made a promise to them!" Ash insisted. "I promised Solgaleo and Lunala that I'd take good care of Nebby. So I'll have to take care of it myself." Nebby was still asleep in Ash's arms, and it happily cooed there.

"Young man," Faba grunted. "Ultra Beasts are far too much of a burden for a little child like yourself to handle, UNDERSTAND?!" He didn't seem to trust Ash at all.

"Now, Faba," Lusamine said, her voice calm and kind.

"You should know," Lillie chimed in, "Ash is not only an extremely strong Trainer, but he also received a Z-Ring and Z-Crystal directly from Tapu Koko."

"From Tapu Koko?" Lusamine said.

"Melemele's Island Guardian!" said Wicke. "Wow!"

"Professor, is that true?" asked Professor Burnet.

"Yeah," Professor Kukui replied. "Our Ash is quite the promising young Pokémon

Trainer! He's already won grand trials on both Melemele and Akala islands!"

"I'm impressed," Lusamine said. She glanced over at Ash. Nebby was now awake and giggling in his arms. Pikachu was perched on Ash's shoulder and was playing with Nebby. "Ash can handle this."

"That's amazing!" Lillie said, proud of her friend.

"But, Lusamine!" Faba protested, his face crumpled with disgust. "You can't!"

"Frankly," Lusamine added, "I'd like to know why Solgaleo and Lunala entrusted little Nebby to your care. And Ash, if you run into any kind of trouble, I'd like you to contact me," she said. "You will, right?"

"Right!" Ash promised.

Nebby yawned, already tired after its

short play with Pikachu.

"It's asleep again," Ash said with a laugh.

"It's so cute when it sleeps," Lillie said.

From close by in Ash's backpack, Rowlet snored.

"Here we go ..." Rotom Dex said anxiously. "We have enough chronic oversleepers at home as it is!"

But with everything they had learned about Ultra Beasts, Nebby, and all the ancient legends and auras, it didn't seem like this crew would have many lazy mornings in their future. Ash and his friends did not know what their next adventure would be, but they were ready!

CHAPTER 5

TEAM ROCKET

"Here we go," Ash said. Nebby sat on his lap. It was breakfast time, and Ash was feeding the little Pokémon by hand. "Now, open wide." Ash popped a piece of purple star candy into its mouth. "Yummy?"

"Ready, Ash?" Professor Kukui asked.

"We'd really better get going."

Ash stood up and started to gather his things. Rowlet hopped into its favourite spot in Ash's backpack.

"Don't forget your lunch," Professor Kukui reminded him, holding up the zippered pouch.

As Ash reached for his lunch, Nebby hurtled its way into his backpack and threw him off balance. Even though Ash loved taking care of Nebby, he was still getting used to it. The other Pokémon in the house needed time to get used to Nebby, too. Nebby always pestered the others while they were eating. Nebby just wanted attention, but they wanted to eat!

There was so much they didn't know about the young Pokémon … or was Nebby

an Ultra Beast? Was it a Pokémon *and* an
Ultra Beast? They all had so much to learn!

Ash glanced over his shoulder at his
backpack. "Looks like you two are having
fun," Ash said to Rowlet and Nebby. "Be
nice to each other." Once they were settled,
Pikachu jumped on Ash's shoulders. It was
nice to have Pikachu there, in its usual

perch. Ash and Pikachu had been through so much together! No matter how many things changed, Ash knew he could always rely on Pikachu.

"Shall we hit the road?" Professor Kukui asked.

Ash nodded. He turned to the Pokémon that were staying at the bungalow. "Lycanroc! Litten!" Ash called out. "Make sure you watch the house!" Lycanroc, the Wolf Pokémon, replied with a happy bark. Litten, the Fire Cat Pokémon, gave a deep, fierce growl. With those two watching out, the house would be safe!

Meanwhile, Ash's rivals were back on Melemele Island. It seemed like Team

Rocket was never far from Ash and Pikachu. It also seemed like the members of Team Rocket were never up to any good. Jessie, James, Meowth and Wobbuffet always had a rotten plan, and they always wanted to catch Pokémon that did not belong to them!

However, today they were working in a food truck selling malasadas – a kind of fried dough, a lot like doughnuts. They smelled amazing!

"Get a lip-smacking taste of our yummy Bewear Brand Honey Malasadas!" James called from the truck window. "They're honey-licious!" The aroma carried on the sea breeze, but no one was buying the yummy pastries. The members of Team Rocket had been camped out in the food truck all morning, and they had not had any customers.

"What a bore!" Jessie complained. She had just been on an online call with a new contact at Team Rocket headquarters, and was frustrated with her. "She's such a broken record! So annoying! She brings up old news, AND WON'T LET IT GO!"

"We're in trouble with the boss because we went to Kanto without getting permission from headquarters," James said. Team Rocket was always trying to please their boss. "So we need to save face and replenish our operating funds, at the very least." Team Rocket was taking a break from Pokémon stealing, by working in the food truck to make money to pay back their boss.

James returned his attention to the deep

fryer, and pulled out a fresh batch of malasadas. "They're perfectly golden brown!" James exclaimed. He hoped people would buy them.

As luck would have it, Team Rocket did have a potential customer. It was Ash, of all people! Ash could smell the sweet aroma, and his stomach was growling. He looked to Professor Kukui hopefully. "They've got honey on them!" Ash pointed out. His mouth watered.

"So! Looking for an early morning snack, are you?" Professor Kukui asked.

"Uh ... if I don't have one, I'll be starving by lunch," Ash claimed. As he stood there, staring at the tasty treats, Nebby floated out of his backpack. Then Nebby landed right on Ash's head – right in front of Team Rocket.

"That's because you didn't eat breakfast!" Rotom Dex reminded him. Rotom Dex was a firm believer that breakfast was the most important meal of the day.

"You'll be fine," Professor Kukui assured him, and he nudged Ash away from the food truck. They all headed towards the

Pokémon School.

Team Rocket stared at their old rival. But they were not upset that Ash didn't buy a treat from their truck. They were excited about something else. "Did you see that?" Jessie whispered.

"How could I not?" James replied, his eyes gleaming.

"That Pokémon must be incredibly rare," Jessie said.

"A purple body? Check. Gaseous features? Check. A rarer-than-rare Pokémon means one thing. And luckily for you, *I* know what that thing is!" James was very sure of himself.

"What is it?" Jessie asked, her voice full of hope and greed.

"A Proto-Koffing!" James declared.

"Proto-WHAT-ing?" Jessie had never heard that word.

"Just as Pikachu evolves from Pichu, I'm certain that *that* Pokémon is Koffing's pre-evolved form, Proto-Koffing!" James explained. Based on Nebby's appearance, James was sure that Nebby was the pre-evolved form of the purple Poison Gas Pokémon. Team Rocket was right about one thing: Nebby was extremely rare.

"Well, word up! When you start flinging facts with such confidence, I'm in!" Meowth stated.

"*This* is our chance to save face with grace!" Jessie declared. "By catching Proto-Koffing!"

"Woo, woo!" James and Meowth

exclaimed. They all wanted to get on their boss's good side again. If they stole Nebby from Ash, they wouldn't have to sell one more malasada! Team Rocket could give Nebby to their boss, and they would be his favourite crew of no-good minions once again.

CHAPTER 6

DISAPPEARING ACT

Of course, Ash had no idea of
Team Rocket's evil plans! He was trying to
concentrate on Professor Kukui's lesson.
But Ash was much better at battling with
Pokémon than sculpting with clay.

"Now, class? Today, you're going to sculpt

your Pokémon partner," Professor Kukui told his group of students. "Closely observing it while you work might lead you to discover something new."

"Right!" all the students replied from their desks. They started shaping the blocks of greenish-grey clay.

"Let's see, who should I make?" Ash wondered out loud. "Nebby and Rowlet are

asleep, so Pikachu, I choose you!"

"*Pika, pika!*" Pikachu was happy to volunteer!

"Now stay perfectly still," Ash requested. All his classmates were focused on their Pokémon as well. Mallow on Steenee. Sophocles on Togedemaru. Lillie on Snowy. Kiawe on Turtonator. And Lana on Popplio, who was trying hard to hold a

bubble-making pose, but the bubble ended up popping all over Lana and her desk!

Some of the students were more gifted sculptors than others.

"It looks more like a Mimikyu. Not a Pikachu," Professor Kukui told Ash honestly. With a lopsided head and jagged mouth, the sculpture did look like Mimikyu!

Sophocles was struggling, too. "Aww ... I think it looks more like a Jigglypuff. Let's see ... hmm ..." He pinched at the pointy ears and tweaked the cheeks. "Not quite as much of a Jigglypuff now," he assessed.

Everyone was concentrating very hard, and no one noticed Nebby was awake. Not only was Nebby awake, it was wandering around the room! Nebby crawled along, winding its cloud-like arms along the floor. When it reached Sophocles's desk, Nebby grabbed his ankle. All at once, Sophocles disappeared!

"*Toge?*" Togedemaru stared at Sophocles's empty seat, confused. A moment later, Sophocles was back.

"What happened?" Sophocles exclaimed. He sounded shocked.

"What's wrong?" Professor Kukui asked.

Sophocles didn't know what to tell the professor. He wasn't sure what had happened! "You know, I thought I just saw a Jigglypuff," he said, knowing it sounded silly.

"I only see Togedemaru," replied Professor Kukui. No one thought any more about it.

A few minutes later, Mallow wondered aloud to herself, "So which pose am I supposed to use? Hmm … what would Oranguru think?" But before Mallow could decide, she disappeared in a shimmering light … then reappeared almost instantly!

"What's up?" Ash asked, sensing the excitement. No one noticed as Nebby cruised its way from one desk to another. Next, it headed toward Lana.

"Mallow disappeared, then reappeared!"

Lana said to Ash. "Like a wave!" At that moment, Lana vanished! When she returned, she was sopping wet. She opened her mouth, and out came a spurt of water – just like a fountain!

"Lana, what happened to you?!" Ash yelped.

"I was in the ocean," Lana replied.

"What's with Nebby?" Ash asked, finally noticing the young Pokémon. Nebby was scuttling over toward Kiawe. Nebby grasped Kiawe's leg, and – like magic – they both vanished!

"Where'd Kiawe go?!" Ash cried.

"HOT!" Kiawe screeched when he reappeared. His hair was smouldering like hot coals!

"Quick, Popplio! Bubble Beam!" Lana

ordered, and Popplio aimed a stream of fresh water at Kiawe's flaming head.

"What just happened to me?!" Kiawe blurted. "I almost fell into a volcano!"

"Volcano?" Ash wondered.

"Did you see that? Nebby disappeared and reappeared with Kiawe," Mallow pointed out. They looked at Nebby, who was floating just above the ground. It toddled around, like nothing unusual had happened.

"That was Teleport!" Rotom Dex declared.

"What's Teleport?" Ash asked, looking from Nebby to Rotom Dex and back again.

"Teleport allows the user to instantly travel from one location to another!" Rotom Dex explained.

"Awesome! I didn't know you could do that, Kiawe!" Ash said, amazed.

"Of course I can't," Kiawe insisted, his hair still sizzling.

"You know what? I think Nebby might have done it," said Lillie.

"Nebby can do that?" Ash said, trying to grasp what that would mean.

"So … where did Nebby go, anyway?" Sophocles wondered.

"Lillie!" Mallow called out, just as Nebby reached for Lillie's leg.

"Maybe Lillie's gonna Teleport!" Ash said. But instead of teleporting Lillie somewhere, Nebby fell fast asleep. What a relief!

While they ate lunch, the classmates tried to figure out how Nebby's Teleport power worked. Ash wished that Nebby had taken *him* somewhere exotic, too.

"So I can't help wondering," Lillie began, "where did everybody go?"

"I went to Jigglypuff's place," Sophocles answered.

"And I went to Oranguru's place," said Mallow.

"I went to the ocean," Lana said.

Kiawe told them he landed on the rim of an active volcano.

"Just a sec. At the moment you were teleported … did your thoughts have anything to do with where you ended up?" Lillie asked her friends.

"Now that you mention it, I thought my sculpted Togedemaru looked more like a Jigglypuff," Sophocles admitted.

"Oh yeah. At that exact moment, I was wondering what Oranguru would've thought about Steenee's pose," Mallow told them.

They all knew that Lana thought about the ocean *all the time*.

"I was thinking about the mountain on Akala Island!" Kiawe confirmed.

"Then it seems to me that the logical conclusion of this mystery is that Nebby must have been reading whatever was on your minds and then teleported you there," Lillie suggested.

"You know, that might just be exactly what happened!" Professor Kukui said.

"Since Nebby is still so little, it's possible that it hasn't decided where it wants to be,"

Mallow suggested.

"That makes a lot of sense!" agreed Lillie.

"Nebby … where do you wanna go?" Ash wondered, lifting the snoozing Nebby into his arms. It looked so sweet and cosy, but Nebby woke up and immediately started to wail. Ash tried to guess what was upsetting the little Pokémon. "Maybe you're hungry! Here, open wide," Ash said, but when he flicked the star candy, it didn't land in Nebby's mouth. It bopped it right above the eye. "Sorry, Nebby!" Of course, Nebby kept crying.

"If I make a funny face, maybe it will stop!" Lana suggested. "It worked on my sisters." Next, they all took turns, trying to make silly faces that would amuse Nebby. They stretched out their mouths and squinted their eyes and stuck out their tongues. Finally, Lillie made Nebby stop crying with the most bizarre face ever!

The little cloud-like Pokémon could be so much work! Ash breathed a sigh of relief. With Nebby, it was always an adventure …

And, just like that, Ash, Pikachu and Nebby vanished!

CHAPTER 7

TEAM ROCKET RETURN

It was Teleport. Nebby finally used it on Ash!

The next thing Ash knew, they were in Jigglypuff's place, and – oh no! – Jigglypuff was singing. Instantly, Ash, Pikachu and

Nebby fell fast asleep. Jigglypuff had the power to send someone to lullaby land with its smooth singing, but it always ended up annoyed!

"*Jiggly-PUFF!*" Jigglypuff scowled at its slumbering visitors and pulled out its marker. How could they sleep through such a gorgeous melody? "*Jiggly, jiggly, jiggly, PUFF, PUFF, PUFF!*" A pair of drawn-on glasses and a thick black-marker moustache would serve them right! It was a classic Jigglypuff prank!

A short while later, the three unexpected guests woke up. "We must've fallen asleep!" Ash exclaimed, looking around. Then he saw Pikachu's extra-thick black whiskers. Pikachu noticed the black lines scrawled all over Ash's face. Jigglypuff had struck again,

wreaking revenge with its handy craft supplies. "We need to wash up," Ash said.

Nebby agreed. Teleport! In the next instant, they were all dunked into the ocean. "I wanted to wash up, but not here!" Ash shouted, still underwater.

Teleport! Before they knew it, they were all in Oranguru's place. The Normal- and

Psychic-type Pokémon was surprised to see them there.

Teleport: next stop, Professor Kukui's bungalow!

Lycanroc's and Litten's hair stood on end, they were so shocked when Ash and the others showed up!

"Oh, wow!" Ash said, seeing his Pokémon companions. "I think we're back home. It's good to see you two!"

A moment later, they appeared at the edge of a volcano. "This has to be Teleport," Ash said. "Man, is that hot!" He yelped, then lost his balance! Ash stumbled and dropped headfirst towards the lava.

"*Pika! Pika!*"

Nebby reached into Ash's mind and found a thought from very early in the day.

As they all fell towards the fiery lava in the volcano, Nebby used Teleport to take Ash and Pikachu somewhere else. It wasn't as hot, but it was still dangerous.

While Nebby had been practising Teleport, Team Rocket had been coming up with a plan. They had abandoned their spot just outside the school. Now they were parked at a nearby beach. They needed some peace and quiet to really think.

"Now hear this!" Jessie declared. "No bob cut, glasses-wearing goon gal is going to defeat ME!" She really did not like the boss's new second-in-command.

"Yeah," said Meowth. "Spoken like a true hothead."

"*Wobbuffet,*" the Psychic-type Pokémon agreed.

"Thanks, I needed that," Jessie replied. "So? That unknown Pokémon – that early Proto-Koffing – needs to be caught. Suggestions?"

"How about an ambush?" said Meowth.

"Staking out the school?" James asked. They had seen Ash take Nebby into the Pokémon School that morning. James knew it would be impossible to sneak into the school without someone noticing them. The place was crawling with teachers and students full of goodwill, who all wanted to keep Pokémon safe and happy. "Keep in mind that the twerps could get in our way at a moment's notice."

"Point taken," Jessie responded. "If only

they'd appear on a desolate beach like this. That would make Pokémon pilfering that much easier."

As if Jessie had had a magical wish granted, at that moment, a ragtag crew appeared at the edge of that very beach.

"Hey, now where are we?" Ash mumbled. All the Teleport action had made him dizzy! He glanced around and saw Team Rocket looking at them like they were a tasty dessert. "Hey, it's you guys!" he shouted.

"A little knowledge is a dangerous thing," replied Jessie.

"And grasping the obvious has that familiar Twerp ring!" James added.

"Team Rocket, let's fight!" Jessie and James said in unison. Meowth and

Wobbuffet were at their sides.

"All right, I wanna know what you're doing here, got it?" Ash demanded.

"I want to know why you're such a lamebrain, get it?" Jessie snarled.

"We're here to help!" James claimed. He tried his best to sound kind and innocent. "That Proto-Koffing you're holding, we'll take it off your hands!"

"Proto-Koffing?" Ash replied.

"The Pokémon in your arms," James said.

"You've got to be out of your mind!" Ash exclaimed. Ash, of course, did not think of Nebby as an earlier Evolution of Koffing. Still, he was not going to tell Team Rocket that Nebby might be something far more rare than a Proto-Koffing. He was not going to reveal that Nebby might be an

Ultra Beast!

"*Pika, pika!*"

"Oh yeah? Not *this* mind," said Jessie, as she pulled out a Poké Ball. At once, Mimikyu appeared. "Case in point. Terrorise the twerp!" Jessie ordered Mimikyu to attack.

Pikachu and Mimikyu started to taunt

each other.

"Say," James began. "I had a thought."

"You *think*?" Jessie said.

"Prove it," Meowth demanded.

Team Rocket huddled together and James explained his idea.

"That was some thought!" Meowth complimented James.

"Thanks! So that's the plan," James confirmed. He then looked over to Ash and his companions. "Let's fight fair and square, man to twerp," he said.

"And we'll be keeping an eye out for dirty tricks," Meowth added.

"Now, Mimikyu, make those lame losers see stars!" Jessie directed.

"Be careful, Pikachu!" Ash warned. "Mimikyu's powerful!"

"*Pika, pika!*" Pikachu promised.

"This could be dangerous, Nebby, so stay back," Ash told his young friend, placing it on the sand.

Nebby lingered just behind Ash as Pikachu and Mimikyu started to face off.

"Pikachu, use Electro Ball!" Ash called out. Pikachu created a ball of pure energy and flung it at Mimikyu, who batted it right back with its zigzag tail. The ball hit Pikachu in the gut.

Mimikyu was as tricky as usual.

"It's going to make it hard to land an attack!" Ash declared. "Wait for an opening and then let 'em have it."

"Now what's the problem?" Jessie asked. "So many to choose from ..."

Ash and Pikachu began to pace in a circle, assessing Jessie and Mimikyu. The Team Rocket contenders did the same. As they paced, Ash and Pikachu moved closer and closer to the food truck. Nebby floated just behind them.

Then, suddenly, Jessie shouted, "There's our chance! NOW! Grab it!"

Meowth darted out from behind the food

truck and snatched Nebby into his outstretched paws. "Consider it grabbed!" Meowth said with confidence. He blew on his claws.

"No, Nebby!" Ash cried.

"You lose, twerp!" Jessie chided. "Proto-Koffing now has a new family!"

"*Wobbuffet.*"

"'New family?' What happened to a fair-and-square fight?" Ash questioned.

"Once a twerp, always a twerp!" James announced. "We fooled you!"

Ash couldn't believe it. The worst part was that Nebby just floated there, in the middle of Team Rocket, like it was happy with its new crew.

"Heads up," James called to the rest of Team Rocket. "This is when we need to be on our guard. You-know-who always shows up around this time." James was worried about Bewear, and he had good reason to be. That Strong Arm Pokémon had a habit of showing up and carting Team Rocket back to its den. It seemed to be very fond of the members of the team.

"Yeah, on cue," Meowth agreed. But even though all the Team Rocket members were thinking about Bewear and were prepared for its arrival, the great pink Pokémon did not show up.

Nebby giggled happily.

Then – Teleport!

Team Rocket landed right in the clearing outside Bewear's den!

"Wait. This makes no sense whatsoever!" Jessie protested. Then the Strong Arm

Pokémon happily lifted the four Team
Rocket members into a bear hug.

"Par for the course," James mumbled.

"We're off with a new blast," Team Rocket
mumbled, as they always did when Bewear
spoiled their plans. Bewear carried them
into its cave.

Meanwhile, Nebby was hidden in the

bushes on the forest floor. All alone, it flipped through its memories of all the places it had teleported that day. When it found the image of the sandy beach where it had left Ash and Pikachu, Nebby teleported again. *Poof!*

"Nebby!" Ash was so relieved that Nebby was safe! "Thank goodness! I was so worried you wouldn't come back!"

"*Pika, Pikachu.*" Pikachu had been worried, too.

Nebby cooed in Ash's arms, feeling cosy. "I know you had quite a day," he said, holding it close. Nebby cuddled up to Ash and fell asleep.

"I found them! Over there!" Kiawe called out. Ash's classmates hurried across the beach to join him. They were all out of breath by the time they reached Ash and the others.

"Ash!" Mallow said. "We've been looking for you!"

"Hi, Nebby!" said Lillie, but Ash quickly hushed her.

"Aw, Nebby's sleeping," Lana observed.

"It used Teleport a lot," Ash explained, looking down at the tiny, cloud-like Pokémon. "It took us to the top of a huge volcano, under the sea, Oranguru's place, Jigglypuff's place."

"Wait," Lillie began, "isn't that ..."

"Right," said Ash. "It's exactly where you guys went. Maybe it wanted to go again, you know? It was even able to come back all by itself." Ash didn't tell them about how Nebby was able to transport Team Rocket and then escape as well.

"Wow," Mallow said.

"Bit by bit, Nebby's getting better and better at using Teleport," Rotom Dex stated. "I'm proud of it."

"We'd better tell Professor Kukui right away!" Sophocles pointed out.

"Yeah, he's probably running all over the forest looking for Ash," Kiawe said.

"That's not good!" Ash exclaimed, forgetting to keep his voice down. Nebby stirred in his arms.

"It's awake!" Rotom Dex cried.

Startled, Nebby threw up its arms and let out a piercing wail. Before the classmates knew it, they were all teleported … to the spire at the very top of the Pokémon School!

Now, it was the all the students who were wailing! "Why did we end up here?" Kiawe yelped. It was a long way down!

"We were thinking about going back to the Pokémon School, weren't we?" Lillie pointed out.

"Sending us to the classroom would've been better than this!" Ash shouted.

"Someone get us down, PLEASE!" cried Sophocles.

The friends grasped onto the spire, and they waited. Eventually, someone would see them. Or Nebby would Teleport them somewhere else!

CHAPTER 8

BATH TIME

A few days later, on a rare lazy morning, Ash decided to give Pikachu a bath. A bath! How soothing! The bubbles and the warm water made having a bath fun and relaxing! All of the Pokémon gathered around to watch.

"*Pika-pikaaaaaa!*"

The bath pail overflowed with suds. Some bubbles rose into the air, and Nebby caught them in its cloud-like arms. "Do you like that?" Ash asked. "They're poofy, like you!" Nebby giggled.

Ash scratched Pikachu behind its velvety ears, and the Electric-type Pokémon closed its eyes.

"*Pika, pika!*"

Litten refused to get close to the sudsy water, but Lycanroc seemed to enjoy watching Ash wash Pikachu. It especially admired how clean Pikachu was at the end. It wasn't a big surprise that Lycanroc wanted a bubble bath, too!

"*Ra-roc!*"

But Rotom Dex was shocked. "A Lycanroc that likes water," it noted as it watched. "And being shampooed, even though it's a Rock-type. Updating data!"

Lycanroc loved the bath as much as Pikachu. It liked to be scratched behind its ears, too, and all around the rocks in its thick mane. It rubbed its nose up against Ash's face, showing Ash lots of love. Its soggy mane dripped all over Ash's shirt.

"Come on, Lycanroc, stop it," Ash said,

trying to shield his face. "You're getting me all wet!" He laughed. "I know that's gotta feel great, right?"

"*Ra-roc.*"

"You're going to be so clean, you'll look cooler than cool," Ash complimented the Rock-type Pokémon. Ash scrubbed Lycanroc's back. Then he put the sponge back in the pail of soapy water. When he pulled it out, there was a big clump of bubbles in his hands. "Look! It's Pikachu! Pretty good, right?"

"It doesn't look anything like Pikachu," Rotom Dex answered, unimpressed.

"All right," Ash said. "Then how about this?" He lifted a fresh blob of suds from the pail. "It's Litten, see?"

"It's the same as before," Rotom Dex

insisted. But Ash was proud of his bubble creation. He wanted Litten's opinion, so he thrust the suds out at the Fire Cat Pokémon.

"Meow!" Ash said.

Startled, Litten screeched and bounded off, pouncing on the edge of the wash pail and splashing the dirty water all over Lycanroc! The dirty water dripped down Lycanroc's face. The Wolf Pokémon's whole body seemed to droop.

"Oh, man!" Ash said with a sigh. "Whoopsy daisy."

"*Pika, pika,*" Pikachu said with sympathy.

"Lycanroc, are you okay?" Ash asked.

Even after it had shaken all the water from its coat, Lycanroc was still filthy!

"Lycanroc! I'll clean you up right away!"

Ash promised, but Lycanroc was angry. Its eyes changed from a cool green to a furious red. "Hold on! Come on, cut it out!" Ash begged.

But Lycanroc barked and growled, threatening Litten. It bared its teeth and sprang. Ash, Pikachu and Nebby had to dodge to get out of the way. Lycanroc

chased Litten all around the garden!
There were yowls and howls, and Ash
couldn't stop it!

Later, when Lycanroc was calm again, Ash
gave it another bath. "Man, that was a
surprise," he admitted. "You got a little too
angry there. I mean, it's not like Litten did
it on purpose."

"I wonder why Lycanroc got so upset,"
Rotom Dex thought out loud.

"You know, I think it got angry because its
mane got dirty," Ash replied. "You'd get
angry too if your Laki wig got dirty, right,
Rotom Dex?"

Ash knew just how to get Rotom Dex to
understand. Rotom Dex loved Detective

Laki so much, and it really liked to wear
the fancy blonde wig. "Right! I get it now!"
Rotom said.

"Lycanroc," said Ash, "I'm really proud of
you. Your Dusk Form is awesome!"

Lycanroc nuzzled up to Ash, feeling
grateful.

"Now stay still! We'll be done in no time,"

Ash said, trying to finish up the bath. "Just hang in there." He kept talking, to try to keep Lycanroc calm. He thought about one of their earlier adventures – the one when they met Lillie's older brother, Gladion. Lycanroc had still been in its Rockruff form back then. "Gladion would be so surprised if he saw you now."

"Ra-roc."

"I wonder what Gladion is up to …" Ash said, curious if the other young Trainer was with Team Skull or working on his own.

At that moment, Nebby floated over to Ash. It giggled and cooed and then placed its cloud-like hand on Ash's shoulder. Pikachu jumped onto Ash's back at once – just seconds before they all disappeared.

"They teleported again!" Rotom Dex

declared, looking at the empty garden. Lycanroc, Pikachu, Ash and Nebby were nowhere to be seen!

Nebby's Teleport landed them in a canyon – in midair! Ash, Lycanroc and Pikachu flailed their arms as they started to fall. A herd of Pinsir was below. The Pinsir did not like it when Ash and the others landed on their backs with a crash!

"Sorry, Pinsir!" Ash cried. Ash, Lycanroc, Pikachu and Nebby raced away in a panic, but the angry Pinsir were hot on their tail. The teeth of the Pinsir gnashed and their claws snapped in anger.

"Use Air Slash!" a voice called out. Suddenly, the air vibrated and shook. The

Pinsir stopped in their tracks and ran off.

Ash stopped to catch his breath. "Oh, man, that was a close one," he mumbled to himself. When the dust cleared, he saw someone he recognised. "Gladion," Ash said, taking a few steps toward Lillie's brother. "Thanks so much!"

Gladion was with his own Lycanroc and an Umbreon.

Then Ash noticed the creature who had actually used Air Slash. "Wow, what is *that*? A Pokémon?" It was nearly as tall as a Charizard. Its body seemed to be a combination of several different animals: the body and hind legs of a panther and the tail of a fish. On its head was a great mask that looked like a fighting helmet.

"*Pika.*" Something about Gladion's

Pokémon made Pikachu anxious.

"I wasn't expecting you to be the one to see it," Gladion replied.

The creature stepped closer to Ash and seemed to be staring down at Nebby. Its growl was like a low, evil wind.

"No way," Gladion said, noticing Nebby. "Is that … ?"

Ash didn't respond. Nebby was wailing far too loud! "Hey, Nebby, please don't cry," Ash begged. "Gladion, could you do something about that Pokémon?" he asked. The creature continued to breathe down Ash's neck.

"It's all right, Silvally," Gladion said, putting his hand on the masked Pokémon's face. "Calm down, it's okay." Hearing Gladion's voice, Silvally took several steps back. Its front feet were like a raptor's.

Pikachu distracted Nebby by making funny faces. Eventually, Nebby cheered up again.

"Thanks a lot, Pikachu," Ash said, and he returned his attention to Gladion.

Gladion observed Nebby closely. "It looks like an Ultra Beast. Am I right?" he asked.

"Whoa," Ash replied. "You know about Ultra Beasts?"

"What is it with you?" Gladion said. "They're really dangerous."

"Nah, it's not dangerous at all," Ash insisted, and he reached out to tickle Nebby's pink belly.

"Then you don't know about Ultra Beasts! You don't have a clue!" Gladion declared.

Gladion obviously thought Ash was being careless. But Ash knew what he was doing – he knew that Nebby was harmless. Didn't he?

CHAPTER 9

PREPARE TO BATTLE

Ash could tell that Gladion was serious.
"Gladion, you have to understand. See, I
made a promise I'd look after it," he tried
to explain. "A promise to Solgaleo and
Lunala."

"What? Solgaleo and Lunala?" Gladion replied, shocked. "The Legendary Pokémon?!"

"Yeah," Ash admitted. "But I made the promise in the middle of a dream." He also had the dream before he had even heard about Ultra Beasts, but he didn't mention that. Now, Nebby was sound asleep in his arms. When it was asleep, it was so peaceful.

Gladion looked at Ash, not sure if he should believe this story of Legendary Pokémon and the foretelling of a strange, cloud-like Ultra Beast.

"Here's what happened," said Ash. "I was just thinking about you earlier. And then Nebby brought us all here."

"You're saying you were teleported?" Gladion asked, still uncertain. "And it was the

Ultra Beast who did it?"

"Well …" Ash said, knowing it sounded impossible. He decided to change the subject. "Hey, I wanted to introduce you to Lycanroc."

Gladion quickly assessed Lycanroc. "It's not a Midnight Form or Midday Form," he pointed out. His own Lycanroc was the

Midnight Form, which stood on its hind legs.

"Yeah, pretty cool, right?" Ash said with pride. "I decided to call it Lycanroc's Dusk Form."

Hearing its own name, Lycanroc smothered Ash with affection. It nuzzled up to him and licked his face. Ash couldn't stop laughing, it tickled so much!

When Lycanroc finally calmed down, Ash looked around. "Where are we?" he asked.

"Ten Carat Hill," Gladion replied. "It's a good place to avoid people."

"Hey, it'd be awesome if you came and visited Lillie once in a while," Ash said. "Lillie's doing really great. You know what? She's managed to be able to touch Pikachu now. She takes good care of Snowy, too."

Gladion seemed to be lost in thought, but Ash kept talking. "You know what else?" he said, looking down at Nebby sleeping in his arms. "Its name is Nebby, and Lillie is the one who named it!"

"Incredible," said Gladion. "Lillie named an Ultra Beast. And she named it Nebby, of all things."

"What do you mean?" Ash asked, trying to follow Gladion's thinking.

Gladion sighed. "Yeah, well I guess it's time you knew." He took another deep breath. "The reason why Lillie couldn't touch any Pokémon for so long … is because she was attacked by an Ultra Beast."

Ash was shocked. He looked at Gladion's face. He could see how the older boy was deep in thought, reliving a painful memory. "I was so scared. There was nothing I could do about it." He shook his head. "But it was ultimately this Silvally who rescued us. Still, Lillie was severely traumatised. She was so afraid, it cast a deep shadow in her heart. And she became unable to touch Pokémon."

Ash was shocked to hear such a horrible story. "She never mentioned it," he said.

"She erased it from her memory," Gladion explained. "It was that terrifying for her. But it won't happen again. I won't let her be terrorised. I'll never let Lillie experience such fear again. I've got to protect her."

Ash could tell that it had been hard on Gladion. It was difficult for him to see his sister to go through something so terrible.

"Look, I'm no longer the same person I once was," Gladion said. Ash assumed he was talking about his time with Team Skull. "I'm a Pokémon Trainer now, and I am dedicated to my Pokémon. We're all getting stronger and stronger! And it's all so I can defeat every last Ultra Beast!" Gladion shook his head. "They bring misfortune to everyone. They should not exist in this world. And Nebby is no exception."

Ash had listened patiently. There was so much about Ultra Beasts that he didn't know, but Gladion had gone too far. "No way!" Ash exclaimed. "Nebby's not like that!"

"How can you know that for sure?"

Gladion questioned. "If Nebby ever showed its true colours as an Ultra Beast, you might be surprised." He paused. "I'll defeat Nebby, no doubt. My Pokémon and me."

"With Silvally?"

"Yes, with Silvally. It was specifically created to defeat Ultra Beasts."

"Created?" Ash repeated, uncertain.

"I can't go into detail," Gladion said, "but no one is to know about it. I've already said too much. You're the one who suddenly appeared while we were training!"

"Sorry, you're right." Ash hadn't meant to just show up. He didn't even know that Nebby was going to Teleport! He had no idea that Gladion was training some special Ultra Beast-fighting machine.

"But there's got to be a reason why an

Ultra Beast would show up here now," Gladion said thoughtfully. "It's important. I need to know why."

"Why?" Ash wondered.

"Who are you, anyway?" Gladion asked.

Ash shrugged. "Who am I? Ash. From Pallet Town."

"Why are *you* the one entrusted with an Ultra Beast?" Gladion questioned. "And what about my mother? Did she agree to all of this? And didn't Solgaleo and Lunala think the Ultra Beast would become dangerous? What's going on here?!" Gladion seemed overwhelmed. He had so many questions! "And a few more things!" he demanded. "What about your Lycanroc? What powers do you possess? What kind of influence do you have on Pokémon?"

"Hold on! Stop it!" Ash said. "I don't have the answers for all that stuff! But I know what we could do instead." Ash looked right at Gladion. "Let's have a battle!"

"A battle?" Gladion repeated. It hardly seemed like the answer.

"You want to learn more about me, right? Then let's have a battle and you can find out!" Ash always loved a battle.

"I'm not seeing the logic in this," Gladion admitted.

"It'll be good for training Silvally!" Ash pointed out. "Don't forget – we never finished our battle before! Team Rocket messed it all up."

"You're right about that," Gladion said.

"What do you say?" Ash asked hopefully. Gladion nodded.

"Awesome! Let's do it!" Ash exclaimed.

It wasn't long before both Ash and Gladion were ready to start the battle. "I'm counting on you, Lycanroc," Ash announced.

On the other side of the field, Gladion was assessing his opponents. "That Lycanroc, what do you think about it?" Gladion asked his own Lycanroc.

The Midnight Form of Lycanroc gave Ash's Lycanroc a long look. "*Lycan.*"

"Yeah," Gladion agreed, focusing on its green eyes. "The eyes show how it's grown."

Umbreon urged Gladion on. That decided it for him.

"All right, then. Let's see how strong you are!" Gladion called out. "Witness the power of the Pokémon with the mask!

Silvally, let's go!"

"Hold on, Gladion," Ash shouted. "This
is the first time Silvally's battling against a
Pokémon who has a Trainer, isn't it?"

"Yes!"

"Ha! All right! Yeah!" Ash cheered,
leaping up and down. "I'm the first!"

"Is that something to be happy about?"

Gladion asked.

"Being the first at anything is always great!" Ash confirmed.

"What a strange kid," Gladion murmured. He really was not sure what Ash was all about.

"Now, let's go, Lycanroc! Rock Throw!" Ash commanded, and Lycanroc blasted a round of rocks at Silvally.

"All right, use Double Hit!" Gladion ordered a counterattack, and Silvally deflected the rocks back in Lycanroc's direction.

"Time to raise your attack power. Now use Swords Dance!" called Gladion, and Silvally seemed to gain some kind of special power.

"Heads up!" Ash warned Lycanroc. "Here it comes!"

"It's all for defeating Ultra Beasts," Gladion said to himself. Aloud, he said, "All right, use Crush Claw!" Silvally's front talons glowed red and it bolted forwards, clapping them together.

Lycanroc bounded out of the way just in time.

"Now, lure it in and then use Bite!" Ash said.

Lycanroc nipped at Silvally again and again. But when it went in for the Bite attack, Lycanroc's jaw clashed with the armoured mask.

"No, Lycanroc!" Ash shouted as the Wolf Pokémon retreated. "It's faster than I thought!" he admitted.

"Use Air Slash!" ordered Gladion, trying to gain an advantage.

"Quick! Use Accelerock!" Ash responded. Lycanroc bolted out of the way with Accelerock and then used it to tackle Silvally head-on. The Synthetic Pokémon skidded backwards, churning up a cloud of dust.

"Pretty good," Gladion said, impressed.

"Offence is the greatest defence!" Ash called out. "Now! Bite, let's go!"

"Double Hit ... NOW!" ordered Gladion.

The two Pokémon collided, and Lycanroc spiralled through the air, landing in the lake in the middle of the canyon. As Lycanroc dragged itself from the lake, it noticed its reflection – soggy, sloppy mane and all. At once, its eyes turned from green to red.

"Oh no! Here we go again," Ash said.

CHAPTER 10

FINAL TEST

Ash was surprised when the Rock-type Pokémon marched out of the water and took its ready stance.

"Wow, you can still battle?" Ash asked Lycanroc. But before Lycanroc answered, it took off, racing towards Silvally at full speed, its teeth bared. It seemed out of control!

"Lycanroc!" Ash called out, as the Pokémon sprang at Silvally again and again.

Gladion observed the battle. "Something's not right. Lycanroc's got work to do," he said. Then he turned to his Midnight Form Lycanroc and Umbreon, who were ready to defend Silvally. "Wait, you two," Gladion advised. "Keep watching."

"Stop! Stop! Stop!" Ash shouted, unable to take it any more. He ran up and threw his arms around Lycanroc, trying to stop its frantic fight.

Pikachu and Nebby watched from the shelter of a tree. Pikachu started to sing,

hoping to comfort Nebby. It was hard to see Lycanroc so upset!

"Come on, Lycanroc," Ash pleaded. "Calm down, please! I'll clean you up, right away."

"It's got growing up to do, too," Gladion said to Ash. "Is this a Dusk Form's true power?"

"I just found out it can get this way!" Ash told Gladion. "Every time Lycanroc's fur gets messed up … it goes crazy! Like that!"

Pikachu was still trying to soothe Nebby. Then, suddenly, Nebby rose up in the air and let out a shrill Supersonic that made everything shake. Ash's ears were ringing and he couldn't feel his feet!

When the sound stopped, all was quiet. And, mysteriously, Lycanroc's fur was clean again!

"Lycanroc! Are you okay?" Ash asked, still worried. "I'm glad you're all clean again. Do you know what? Nebby probably didn't want you to be angry." Lycanroc rubbed its rocky mane up against Ash's face. The Wolf Pokémon looked stunned. "Right," Ash reassured it. "You're fine. There, there."

"What do you wanna do?" Gladion called out. "Do you wanna stop?"

"No way! Let's battle!" Ash shouted. He never liked to back down. "What's done is done. Back to business! Let's go, Lycanroc!"

"Silvally, let's end it with one strike! Use

Swords Dance!" Gladion ordered.

Ash was not going to let them win with a single strike. "Quick, use Accelerock!" Ash directed, and Lycanroc darted forwards. "One more time! Use Accelerock again!"

"Now, Crush Claw!" called Gladion.

This time, Silvally was too fast for Lycanroc. Its talons glowed red, and one swipe of Crush Claw knocked Lycanroc down.

"And that is that," said Gladion when Lycanroc did not get back up. "Return!" With that order, Silvally was safe and resting in its Poké Ball.

Ash, Pikachu and Nebby were checking on Lycanroc. It was tired from the battle.

"It makes sense. I understand," Gladion said, approaching them. "Now I know who

you really are."

"You see? We're just us," Ash replied. "That's all."

"It was a good experience for Silvally," Gladion told Ash. "It's tough for us. You and me."

Ash tried to figure out exactly what Gladion meant.

"With your Lycanroc. And my Silvally," Gladion began to explain. "They both have their very own quirks. Looks like it'll take time until they truly become strong."

"You're right! That's why we should battle more so we get stronger and stronger!" Ash really believed in battling.

"Later," Gladion said, sounding like he thought it was a good idea, too. "But that's right. Please promise me one thing."

Ash paused.

"About seeing me today ... and also seeing Silvally. Don't say a word." Gladion let his words sink in. "Promise me. I ask you because I trust you."

"Got it," Ash agreed, feeling a certain pride in having earned Gladion's trust.

With that, Gladion turned and started

back home with his Pokémon.

"All right! Let's go home, too!" Ash said to his crew. But when he looked at Nebby, he realised that it was sleeping. Nebby was so sweet when it was asleep … but it took Ash a moment to realise that right now, a sleeping Nebby was a problem. "Wait …" he said. "How are we supposed to get home from here? You're asleep! Take us home, Nebby! Please! Please, Nebby! Wake up!"

With Nebby around, Ash's life was becoming more interesting by the day! There were so many questions in his future. Many of them had to do with Nebby and Ultra Beasts. What was Nebby's real nature? What were all its powers? Were there other

Ultra Beasts on the Alola Islands? Ash could not know, at least not yet. But he did know that it was his job to protect Nebby from the likes of Team Rocket ... and maybe worse! He also knew that he had many allies and friends he could rely on. And maybe Gladion was one more.

One thing was clear: Ash's next adventure would be a big one – and he certainly would not go on it alone!

The End

WHICH POKÉMON FROM THE ALOLA REGION DID YOU SPOT IN THIS ADVENTURE?

☐ COSMOG

☐ LYCANROC

☐ POPPLIO

 PIKACHU

 MEOWTH

 SILVALLY

READ ALL THE BRILLIANT

ASH'S BIG
CHALLENGE

POKÉMON PERIL

THE ORANGE LEAGUE

SCYTHER
VS CHARIZARD

RACE TO DANGER

SHOW TIME!

POKÉMON ADVENTURES!

POWER UP PSYDUCK

THE WINNER'S CUP

THE POKÉMON SCHOOL

ALOLAN CHALLENGE

ADVENTURE ON TREASURE ISLAND

OLD FRIENDS NEW BATTLES

Find out about the Pokémon Movies
in the Official Pokémon Ultimate Guide!